CECILIA'S HOUSE & THE FORAGING CLASS

AMERICAN CHAPTERS

GRETA GORSUCH

WAYZGOOSE PRESS

Book Design and Editing by Maggie Sokolik, Wayzgoose Press

Cover Design by DJ Rogers, Book Branders

For Karen

CONTENTS

FROM THE AUTHOR

Welcome to our series, *American Chapters*. The *American Chapters* series presents short stories in vivid and easy-to-read 500-word chapters, perfect for English language learners internationally, and adult literacy learners in countries where English is commonly used.

All *American Chapters* print stories are also offered as audiobooks for learners who want to hear and read the stories and hear the sounds of American English.

American Chapters are lively, relevant, and realistic short stories about living in the United States of America. About Americans, immigrants, sojourners, and the diverse peoples living in this wide landscape, the stories touch on the tough questions, and the great things in life—things like work, ethnic differences, our connections to the past, our place in nature, being new, small town life, personal loss, and above all, new beginnings.

CECILIA'S HOUSE

CHAPTER 1

Cecilia was wondering what to do next. This was typical for her. She had a lot of energy. She had a lot of ideas. She would think of something to do. She planned to do it, and then, she did it.

Any day could look like today: Get up. Start a cake for Frannie. Put the cake in the oven. Pick up trash from the front yard. Water the flowers. Order some new "I Clean It" t-shirts online. Look at her fingernails. What color should she pick this week? Maybe light purple? Was that too bright? Then, take a shower. Put her long brown hair in curlers. Wait ten minutes. Take the curlers out. Brush her hair. Look at her few gray hairs and frown. Put on her make up. Put on a pair of blue jeans, an "I Clean It" t-shirt, an orange and red "Sunflower Roughnecks" team jacket, and a pair of pink socks and shoes. Take Frannie's cake from the oven.

Here it was—8:30 AM. Cecilia was trying to decide if she had time to clean the bathroom before her first cleaning job. She decided she didn't. She wanted to stop by Frannie's house before going to town. Frannie didn't sound good on the telephone last night. If Frannie was sick, Cecilia was going to have a busy day. There were four houses to clean! Cecilia didn't look forward to cleaning them by herself. Frannie was her friend, and Frannie was also her partner in the "I Clean It" house cleaning business.

"What's wrong?" she asked Frannie. She could hardly hear Frannie's answer. Was the cell phone signal that bad?

"I don't know," Frannie said. "It's probably just a cold." She coughed. "It feels like I can't get enough air," she said.

"Is Donny there? Can I talk to him?" Cecilia asked. Donny was Frannie's no-good son. He was 32 years old. He didn't have a regular job.

"No," Frannie said. "He's visiting friends in Houston."

"Uh-huh," Cecilia said. She started planning. What could she do to help? Could she take oranges? Cough syrup? Aspirin? She said, "Do you want me to come over? I have some things that might help."

"No, no," Frannie said. "You'll just catch my cold. This is a bad one. It's been two weeks! But really, forget it. I'll be fine. If I can make it to Mrs. Morris's, I'll see you there."

This morning, though, Cecilia didn't feel good about that phone call. That's why she wanted to stop by Frannie's. How long did Frannie have that cold? Two weeks? *More than two weeks*, Cecilia thought.

Cecilia took the cake and put it in the front seat. She checked her rags and buckets and sprays in the back of her car. She was ready to go. She pulled out onto the highway.

CHAPTER 2

Cecilia liked listening to music. When she was driving a car, listening to music was heaven. She played all sorts of music. Sometimes she played a radio station, KSNF 99.9. It was a little country music station in Sunflower. Sometimes she could get a radio station in Dallas, KDLS 101.3. It was a rock n' roll station.

When Cecilia got tired of the radio, she listened to CDs. Some were rock, some were country. She liked to try new things. Last week she drove an hour to Plainview to a used CD shop. She bought a jazz CD by Thelonious Monk. It was in the "bargain basket."

This morning she listened to jazz for the first time in her life. She didn't know what to think. She couldn't catch the mood of the songs. One song, "Don't Blame Me," sounded so happy. But the song title wasn't happy at all. "Blame" was a strong word. "Blame" sounded like anger and secrets.

Cecilia lived outside of Sunflower, Texas. Sunflower was a small town. In the 1960s, there were 1,400 people in

Sunflower. In the 1980s, 1,000 people were in Sunflower. By the 1990s, many young people were leaving. They weren't coming back. They wanted jobs in Plainview or Dallas. No one wanted to live in a town with only one restaurant and no cafés.

Sunflower was right in the middle of big country. This part of Texas was high and flat and dusty. There were few trees. The sun shone every day. The sky was high and blue. It almost never rained. On some mornings, Cecilia thought she could see for a hundred miles. The towns were far apart. She needed a car to get around.

Cecilia loved Sunflower. She loved the country all around Sunflower. Her father died a few years before. He left her his big green two-story house just outside of Sunflower. She never dreamed of living anywhere else. Her "I Clean It" business was small, but Cecilia thought it was doing OK. Sunflower was getting smaller, but at least twelve people there still wanted their houses cleaned. Cecilia wanted to try her business in other small towns nearby. She had a car. She wanted to grow her business. She was always planning.

Cecilia turned off the main highway to go to Frannie's house. She wanted to listen to "Don't Blame Me" one more time. She pressed the button to play the song again. Just as the song started, she saw something. There were flashing lights in her mirror. They were bright blue, red, and yellow. She pulled off the road. It was the sheriff's car. Then, a second set of lights came up, fast. It was an ambulance. Up ahead, the sheriff's car and the ambulance both turned onto a smaller road. It was Frannie's road. They were going straight to Frannie's house!

Cecilia sat in shock. Then she put her car into *drive*. She pulled back onto the road. She was shaking. Finally, she got to

Frannie's house. She was just in time to see a sheriff's deputy come back outside. The deputy, a woman named Alice Garza, turned off her flashing lights. Cecilia saw Alice Garza's brown deputy's uniform. Alice had on her shiny silver deputy's badge. It was the shape of a star.

CHAPTER 3

Cecilia knew Alice Garza. Alice and Cecilia went to school together. They were both members of the girls' basketball team, the Sunflower Roughnecks. Alice went to college, and Cecilia stayed in Sunflower. Then, Alice came back to Sunflower. "I missed the big sky," she told Cecilia. Their conversation this morning was between old friends.

"Are you OK?" Alice asked.

"I'm not sure," Cecilia. "That depends on what you say about Frannie. But I think I already know. You turned off your lights. Is she dead?"

"Yeah," Alice said. She looked sad. They were quiet for a minute. Then Alice said, "It looks like she's been gone for four or five hours. She was in bed. She looks peaceful. I don't think she was in pain. But, that's for Doc Smithy to say." Doctor Smithy was the last doctor in Sunflower. If someone died, he was called.

Alice said to Cecilia, "Come into the house. I can't let you into the bedroom where Frannie is. But you can still say goodbye to your friend, in a way." Cecilia got out of her car. She went through the front door into Frannie's house.

Frannie's house was a mess. There were rags and clothes and trash on the floor. There were newspapers and books on the sofa. The kitchen sink was full of dirty dishes. Frannie was sick, so the mess wasn't a big surprise. Filled with sadness, Cecilia moved some newspapers aside and sat on the sofa.

Cecilia thought about Frannie for awhile. The two ambulance drivers moved around in Frannie's bedroom. Everyone waited for Doc Smithy to arrive. He came ten minutes later. He followed Alice into Frannie's bedroom. Cecilia could hear them talking.

Frannie's house was not large. There was just the living room, a kitchen, two bedrooms, and one bathroom. This was typical for a small Texas town. Houses built in the 1930s weren't very big. Cecilia saw that the door to Donny's room was open. She walked over and looked in. She needed to contact Donny. Frannie's son needed to know what happened to her. Cecilia didn't have Donny's number on her cell phone. To her surprise, Donny's room was completely empty. There was just a bed. It was neatly made. But there were no clothes, or books, or anything else. When did Donny move out? Frannie never said anything about Donny moving out.

This troubled Cecilia. Why didn't Frannie tell her? They were partners, but also friends. Anyway, Alice Garza might have an idea of how to find Donny. Maybe she could call the police in Houston. They would know how to reach Donny.

Cecilia went back into the living room. She felt uneasy. Frannie had a table in the living room. She called it her "office." This is where Frannie did the money part of their "I Clean It" house cleaning business. On the table was a laptop computer. It was still on. It showed some crazy website called "Las Vegas Poker."

Next to the laptop was a large stack of papers. The one on top was a credit card bill for $4,300. It had "OVERDUE" and "PAY NOW" written on it in red. The next one was a letter from the bank. Cecilia didn't mean to look, but she saw the word "FORECLOSURE" on it. That meant only one thing: Franny was losing her house.

CHAPTER 4

For the first time in many years, Cecilia wasn't planning anything. She wasn't thinking about what to do. She just sat in Frannie's messy living room. There were books and newspapers and unpaid bills everywhere. Cecilia couldn't believe it.

In her last days, Frannie's life was messy, too, it seemed. She was losing her house. She owed a lot of money. Donny, Frannie's son, moved out. How did this all happen? When? Cecilia didn't know.

Alice Garza, the deputy sheriff, called out to Cecilia, "Cecilia. Hey, Cecilia?"

Cecilia looked up. "Yeah?" she said in a low voice.

"Doc Smithy says he's done here," Alice said. "They're taking Frannie to Plainview. There's a funeral home there."

"OK," Cecilia said. Alice took the books off a chair near Cecilia and sat down.

"What's up?" Alice said.

"I'm not sure," Cecilia said. Then she pointed to the stack of bills on the table. "It looks to me like... Frannie was losing this house. It's like she didn't have any money. I don't get it. The house cleaning business is doing OK."

Alice didn't say anything. The two ambulance drivers were taking Frannie out the front door. They would take her to Plainview. Cecilia's eyes followed the white sheet out the front door, out to the treeless yard, out to the ambulance. Its lights were off. The drivers were in no hurry.

Then Cecilia said, "Do you know how to get hold of Donny? He needs to know what happened to his mom."

"It was Donny who called us to check on Frannie," Alice said. "Frannie didn't answer her phone this morning. Donny got worried. So, he called the sheriff's office. I was on duty."

"Oh," Cecilia said.

"Donny told me he moved out three months ago," Alice said. "He was calling her every night to check on her. He's working for an oil company in Houston."

"What?" Cecilia said.

"Yeah," Alice said.

"I had no idea," Cecilia said. "No idea at all." She thought for a minute. Then she said, "Is Donny coming to Sunflower? Someone needs to tell the funeral home people what to do. Someone needs to figure out what to do with all this." She pointed to the house, the bills, and the mess.

"Yeah," Alice Garza said. "He's on his way. It's fourteen hours to drive from Houston."

"Do you have his phone number?" Cecilia asked. Alice did. Cecilia put Donny's number into her phone.

Everyone was gone now. Only Cecilia and Alice were left. Cecilia left Frannie's empty house and drove back home. She had some plans to make.

CHAPTER 5

Cecilia spent the rest of the morning calling people. First, she went down her list of four cleaning jobs for today. She called old Mrs. Morris and told her she would come at three PM. Next, she called Ms. Santos, Mr. Odom, and Mrs. Redfield to tell them about Frannie. She would clean their houses next week. Ms. Santos wasn't home, so Cecilia left a message.

She didn't want to clean houses today, but Mrs. Morris was 89. She lived alone. She didn't have children. She had a sister living in Dallas. Her sister was 93.

Cecilia did more than clean the old woman's house. She checked Mrs. Morris's refrigerator. She wrote down anything Mrs. Morris needed, like milk, bread, or fresh fruit. She made sure Mrs. Morris paid her electric bill. From time to time, she washed clothes for Mrs. Morris. She cleaned the house. She used spray and rags on Mrs. Morris's windows, until they were perfect. Then, she went to the Sunflower Pay Day Supermarket. She bought the things on her list. She took the food back to Mrs. Morris's house.

Sometimes, she picked up a newspaper for her to read. The

Sunflower Reporter still put out a newspaper once a week. She listened to Mrs. Morris's questions. "Was it hot outside? Did it look like rain? Did she enjoy her drive to Plainview? Was that a new color on Cecilia's fingernails?"

Cecilia answered, "No, it's not too hot." And, "No, no rain." And, "Yes, it was OK. I bought some music CDs." "Yes, it's 'Sunset Orange.'"

This morning, Cecilia told Mrs. Morris about Frannie. Mrs. Morris looked sad. She asked, "What happened? Was she sick?"

Cecilia answered, "She had a cold for a few weeks. Dr. Smithy thinks Frannie had some other problems. Maybe her heart."

"Oh," Mrs. Moore said.

It was hard for people in Sunflower to see a doctor. Dr. Smithy only worked part time. He worked only for the town of Sunflower. He came only if someone died. It was his job to make decisions about a death. Was it an accident? Was it a natural death? Dr. Smithy didn't treat living people. To see a doctor, people in Sunflower had to drive an hour to Plainview or to Lubbock. Lubbock was two hours away.

"Well, I'm really sorry," Mrs. Moore said. "Let me know if there is anything I can do."

"Sure," Cecilia said. She picked up her cleaning things. She wanted to go home. She wanted to sit in her own house and watch the evening come. She wanted to listen to music. She didn't want to plan anything. She was too tired.

She put her things in her car. The sun was starting to go down. Mrs. Morris had some tall elm trees in front of her house. They made long shadows in the sunset. Then, Mrs. Morris called from her door. "Cecilia!" she said.

Cecilia went back to Mrs. Morris. Mrs. Morris handed her

a white envelope. It had $300 in it. She said, "I usually give this to Frannie, but now it seems you should get it. It's my monthly payment."

Cecilia counted the cash. She said, "This is too much. It should be $50 for each visit. That's $200, not $300."

Mrs. Morris looked confused. She said, "No, no. That's what I gave Frannie every month. I paid $75 each time."

Cecilia finally said, "OK." Then she handed $100 back. "I only charge $50 per visit. We can talk about it again next week. All right?"

Mrs. Morris nodded and shut her door.

CHAPTER 6

Cecilia cleaned three houses the next afternoon. She had a few hours in the morning to think and plan. She sat in her large, bright kitchen. She was having hot tea. She grew up in this house. It had large windows. There were six rooms upstairs, and eight rooms downstairs. The house was on the main highway. It was set far back. That kept the highway dust and noise away from the house.

For Texas, the house was old. Her grandfather built the house in 1927. Sunflower was a new town then.

Cecilia's grandfather and father both farmed. They did well at it. They found three large water wells on the land. The water was sweet and clear. They had cattle and sheep. They also grew pumpkins. Sunflower was sometimes called "The Pumpkin Capital." Every year, there was a pumpkin festival.

A few years before her father died, he told Cecilia to put in small wind turbines. He said, "I know you don't want to farm. You can lease the land out to Mr. Raynes. He said he wants it for cattle, and maybe pumpkins. You'll get some money from the lease. But, we should put in wind turbines, too. They're costly! But you can power our house with electricity for years to come."

"All right, Dad," Cecilia said.

After six months, there were three new, white wind turbines on the land behind the house. They were small, house-size wind turbines. They had the words "Windspeed" on their sides. "Windspeed" was the name of the company that made them. The Windspeed turbines were forty feet high. They each had three blades, ten feet long. The blades turned and swept the air with a fast *whish whish whish* sound. If the wind blew, they made electricity. Whenever Cecilia walked behind her house, she saw the white wind turbines. She thought about her father. She also thought about change.

Her father taught Cecilia about money. From a young age, he taught her how to make money and save money. He told her how much money he made. He told her what he did with it. "We'll save some of this money for the house. We may need to paint it next year," he said. "This other money, we'll put into school bonds. Plainview wants to build a new school. They're trying to get money for it. So, let's lend them our money to do that."

Cecilia's father was very honest and direct about money. Perhaps this was why Frannie's secret money problems hurt Cecilia so much. Cecilia never thought her business partner would cheat her.

Cecilia called all twelve of her "I Clean It" clients. She learned that Frannie charged them all $75, or even $90 per visit. All this time, she told Cecilia they got $50 per visit. With Frannie and her secrets, Cecilia was making $25 per visit. But Frannie was making $25 or even $40 extra per visit. What was she doing with the money? She didn't spend it on her house. Frannie was losing her house when she died. She wasn't paying her bills. Cecilia just didn't understand it.

Cecilia decided it was time to call Donny, Frannie's son. Maybe he had some answers. Cecilia called Donny's phone. He answered on the second ring.

"Hi, Cecilia," he said. "I thought you might call."

"Hi, Donny," Cecilia said. "Are you in Sunflower yet?"

"Yeah," he said. "I'm at Mom's."

The silence between them went on for ten, fifteen, twenty seconds. Then, Donny said, "I need to talk to you. Are you free sometime this week? Maybe Thursday?"

"Yeah, OK," Cecilia said. "That's the day after tomorrow. Six PM." Without saying "OK" or "goodbye," they both hung up. Their conversation on Thursday would not be easy.

Cecilia spent the afternoon cleaning the Roscoes' little house in Sunflower. Next, she went to Mr. and Mrs. Hernandez's house. They had a large family and two dogs. Their kids were in school, so the house was quiet. The dogs were no trouble. Cecilia liked dogs. She carried dog treats in her pocket. Tonka, their big white dog, followed her everywhere. He wanted a treat. Cecilia had no idea what kind of dog he was. He was like a big, friendly, white hairball.

Finally, around 4:30, Cecilia went to Mrs. Gold's house. Mrs. Gold was like Mrs. Morris. She was old. She needed more than house cleaning.

When Mrs. Gold had a bad day, she wouldn't come out of the bathroom. Cecilia would call through the bathroom door, "Are you OK, Mrs. Gold?" Mrs. Gold sometimes answered, "Yes!" in her little Texas twang. "But I ain't comin' out! My hair don't look right!"

Sometimes Mrs. Gold had good days. Today was a good day. She sat at the kitchen table while Cecilia cleaned. Cecilia checked Mrs. Gold's refrigerator. She washed some of Mrs.

Gold's clothes. They were in a big stack on the floor. If Cecilia wanted to clean the floor, she had to pick up the stack of dirty clothes. When she was done, she joined Mrs. Gold at the kitchen table. Mrs. Gold wanted to pay her bills, but her handwriting was horrible. Her hands shook. She asked Cecilia to write her checks for her. First, they paid the electric bill. Then, they paid the water bill.

Cecilia said, "You only need to pay me $50 for each visit." Mrs. Gold didn't say anything. She just asked Cecilia to write herself a $200 check for the month.

Out of nowhere, Mrs. Gold said, "I heard about Frannie. I'm awful sorry."

"Yes," Cecilia said. "Thank you."

"Sometimes I worry," Mrs. Gold said. "What if I end up like Frannie? Bein' alone in a house. No one knowin' or carin' if I'm OK."

"Well, you have me," Cecilia said. "I care if you're OK."

"Why thank you. But I wonder, could you come twice a week? Just to clean, and make sure I'm OK?" Mrs. Gold asked. Her eyes were large and blue behind her glasses.

Cecilia thought about it. "Well, I guess so," she said. "I can come Tuesday and… what about Saturday afternoon?"

"All right," Mrs. Gold said. "I can pay you $150 per week."

Cecilia finally agreed to take $150 per week, and then she left. She wondered about Mrs. Morris and Mrs. Gold. She wondered how they ended up alone. Both of them were married at one time. Their husbands died. Like Cecilia, they didn't want to leave Sunflower. They had happy memories there.

Mrs. Gold had children, but they never called. One was in Wichita Falls. Cecilia didn't know where the other one was. Cecilia thought that maybe her own future wasn't any different. She never married and never had kids. At 39, she might never do either of those. Who would she leave her home to? What sort of family would live there?

When Cecilia got home, she pulled a chair into her back yard. She watched the three wind turbines in the distance. They flashed in the sunshine. Cecilia sat in her chair. She could see the cloud shadows race over the field behind her house. The farmer who leased her land was beginning spring planting for pumpkins. He had a farm crew of five people. They planted pumpkin seeds in rows. The rows stretched far into the distance. It was good land. If they had some rain, the pumpkins would do well.

CHAPTER 8

The next day Cecilia didn't have any houses to clean. Cecilia spent the time thinking about the "I Clean It" business. She wondered about changing the business. She could change from just house cleaning to looking after old people in their homes—people like Mrs. Morris and Mrs. Gold. Sunflower had a small nursing home. Most people didn't have money for that. Most people didn't want to be in a nursing home, either. If their health was good, they wanted to stay at home. They wanted their own things around them. They wanted to keep their books, their pets, their dishes, and their photographs of loved ones. Cecilia could help them do that.

Cecilia wanted to expand her business to other small towns. The little town of Lockney was nearby. Ralls was, too. They had a lot of older people. Their kids moved away to cities like Dallas or Lubbock. That left a lot of old people alone in their houses.

Cecilia needed to do more thinking and planning. It was a big change. She needed to learn more. Maybe she could take some classes on home health care. Maybe she should get a license. She would need that if her clients wanted her to handle their money. People needed to trust her. Frannie cheated her and their clients, too. That really hurt Cecilia. Her father was honest, and so was she. She still couldn't understand why Frannie did what she did.

Cecilia decided to stay busy that day. She did her best thinking when moving around. She washed her clothes, and then her sheets. She hung them outside to dry. The spring day was warm and still. The Windspeed wind turbines were not moving at all. That was strange. Usually the blades turned: *whish whish whish*. The stillness in the air made Cecilia think a storm was coming. Sometimes they got storms in the spring, but not this year. They needed rain.

She cleaned all the rooms downstairs. She vacuumed and sprayed and wiped. She swept the wood floors. They were golden and smooth. Cecilia thought they might be pine. In the summer Cecilia enjoyed walking barefoot on the cool wood. She washed the inside windows at the front of the house. The front of the house faced west. In the afternoons, the sun shone strongly. She went out to clean the outside windows.

As she wiped, a breeze came out of the southwest. It was cool. She turned to look behind her. To her surprise, she saw gray clouds piled high in the sky to the southwest. The sky was clear only an hour before. Cecilia walked between the trees in her front yard to see better. They had only small spring green leaves. Some rain would be good for them.

The gray clouds got closer. Cecilia saw a long, long curtain of rain under the clouds. Cecilia ran to get her sheets from the back yard. There was more cool wind, and a rumble of thunder. Cecilia got inside with her sheets just as the rain started.

She piled the sheets on her sofa. She went to the front windows to watch the storm.

It rained all night. Cecilia woke up to the sound of rain at one AM. She woke up again at four AM and it was still raining. It was a good sound. There was nothing better than being in a good house with the sound of rain outside.

CHAPTER 9

The next morning, the gray clouds were gone. The morning sky was clear and soft. Cecilia could see the three white wind turbines turning behind her house.

Cecilia had four houses to clean today. The houses were no trouble. All of them were in Sunflower. They belonged to people who were at work all day. A few had to drive ninety minutes or more to Lubbock to work. Cecilia never saw those clients. They left at six AM and got home at seven or eight PM.

Cecilia visited the post office and the bank. She sat in the tiny city park for an hour, waiting for six PM. The few trees in the city park looked good. That long night of rain came just in time. To her surprise, she saw a new sign on an empty old building. It said:

LINDA'S RESTAURANT AND CAFE
OPENING SOON!

Sunflower could use a café.

Then, she drove over to Frannie's house. Donny was waiting for her. Frannie was only gone for two days. But the house looked empty, already. Donny was inside. He was putting trash into trash bags. He was cleaning the house out.

"Well, Donny, this is a sad day," Cecilia said from the doorway.

Donny looked up. He was a short man, and thin. He looked like Franny that way. But he also looked different today. He looked sad, older. His brown hair was cut short. He wore nice clothes. He looked like he spent time inside. He looked good. Suddenly Cecilia felt very shy. She was wearing an old "I Clean It" t-shirt. Her hair and nails looked horrible.

"Hey, Cecilia," he said. Donny looked at Cecilia's face. Then he said, "Let's sit out front." He found two chairs and carried them outside. The sunshine was bright. A few passing clouds went over. For a few seconds at a time, it was dark and cool.

"So, when did you move out?" Cecilia asked. "Frannie never told me."

"That sounds like her," Donny said. "Everything became a secret for her. She kept me in the dark too, it turns out. Well, Mom and I had a bad fight. This was about three months ago. I got a call about an oil job in Houston, and so I went." Cecilia didn't say anything. Then Donny said slowly, "Mom had a gambling addiction. That's what we were fighting about."

Cecilia just look at him. Frannie had a *gambling addiction*? *What?* Of course. This must be where all her money went. She was gambling away her money. That was why she cheated Cecilia. That was why she cheated her "I Clean It" clients, like Mrs. Moore, too. That was why she was losing her house. That was why she lost her son, Donny. Cecilia felt such empty blackness.

She said to Donny, "How did she do it? Did she go to a casino?"

He said, "She did her gambling online. You saw her laptop?"

"Yeah," she said. "It was still on the morning they found her. Some 'Las Vegas poker' website."

Donny looked sad. He couldn't talk for a minute. Cecilia looked away. More empty blackness. It was horrible.

"Anyway," he said, "I didn't notice until she started losing big money. She didn't pay her bills one month. They were in a stack on her table. I was doing some work in Sunflower on a road crew. So, I paid the bills. I just thought the "I Clean It" business wasn't doing well. Then once, when she was out of the house, the phone rang. It was a credit card company. Mom got a new credit card. She was already above her limit by $3,000. I couldn't understand why she needed another credit card. When she got home, I asked her about it. She said the man on the phone was wrong. She didn't have any credit cards. I knew she was lying. I found the gambling websites on her laptop. I kept asking her about her bills and her laptop. Finally, she started screaming at me. She said I had no right to her life. If she wanted to gamble, she could."

Neither Cecilia nor Donny said anything for a while. They watched the clouds pass by in the sky. Then, Donny told her about his new job in Houston. He left Sunflower. He called Frannie every night to check on her. She usually answered, but she didn't want to talk.

"I guess she wanted to get back to her online gambling," he said.

Then Cecilia told Donny about the "I Clean It" clients. She told him about Frannie charging too much money and keeping the extra money.

"More and more secrets," Donny said. "Maybe she had a heart attack. I don't know. Maybe her secrets killed her."

He went inside the house. He came out with a folded piece of paper. "I found this on the table," he said. "It's from Mom, to you. It's her handwriting."

He gave it to her. Cecilia read the note. It said:

Cecilia,

*I want you to have my house. Donny doesn't want it. He
doesn't belong in Sunflower anymore.
Please don't blame me. Maybe my house can pay you
back somehow.*

Love, Frannie

"Well," Cecilia said, "that's not going to happen. It's your
house, not mine. You have a right to it. I don't know how
much she owed on it. It might not be that much. Why don't
you pay it off? You keep it. You'll have a place to stay if you
come back to Sunflower."

"I checked with the bank," Donny said. "She owed $17,000
on it. I paid it off this morning."

Cecilia had no idea what to say.

Donny said, "I like Houston. I like my job there. I won't be
coming back to Sunflower. There's nothing here for me."

Cecilia said, "Don't say that just yet. You don't know how
you'll feel in a year or two. Keep the house."

"OK," Donny said, after a very long silence.

Cecilia got up. She said, "Let's go inside." She was making
plans.

"Why?" Donny asked.

"Two things. First. We need to find something for your
mother to wear for her funeral. I know what her favorite dress
was," Cecilia said. "Second. Let's wipe the memory off of
Frannie's laptop computer."

"I didn't think of that," Donny said.

"It might make you feel better," Cecilia said.

They went inside. It took Donny twenty minutes. Both
Donny and Cecilia cried. They wiped the memory on the

laptop clean. They took off all the applications. It was no longer a gambler's laptop. It could be used for anything. It no longer had any secrets.

CHAPTER 11

In two days, Frannie would be buried in the Sunflower Pioneer Cemetery. Donny said he was going to Plainview to plan the funeral. He told Cecilia to call if she needed anything. She said she would. They spent a few more hours cleaning the house. Cecilia told Donny about a bargain store in Ralls he could take Frannie's things to.

"Be careful what you give away. Don't be in a big hurry," Cecilia said. "Sometimes a dish or a book will bring you good memories of someone."

Donny gave Cecilia a wooden chair. It was large and smooth, and nice to sit in. It was from Germany. It was a wedding gift from Donny's father to Frannie. Frannie never gave it up, even when she needed the money. Cecilia took the chair. She wondered where to put it in her house. Maybe she would put it in the front hall, where the western sun glowed bright. That was just the spot.

It was getting dark when Cecilia drove home. She took the long way, all around Sunflower. Her mood was quiet. There wasn't a better word for it. She saw trees and grasses becoming green after the rain. Some farmers were out looking at their fields. At least one field of pumpkins had come up. The little pumpkin plants were only an inch high.

Far off in the distance toward Lockney, Cecilia saw something new. She saw seven new white wind turbines. These were not house-type wind turbines, like her small Windspeed turbines. These new wind turbines were huge. Their large white blades turned slowly in the sunlight. Cecilia smiled. Sunflower might be getting smaller, but it wasn't dying. Change was coming all the time. She wanted to be here, in this bright beautiful world, and see those changes.

She listened to "Don't Blame Me" again on her CD player. Did she blame Frannie? Was she angry with her for lying? For taking money that wasn't hers? If someone had an addiction, did you blame them for what they did? Cecilia decided it didn't matter. What did matter was that Frannie's actions hurt other people. It would take time for Cecilia to remember Frannie with friendship. She also believed that in time she would remember her friend in better days.

Cecilia got home as the sun slipped away into the west. She got out of her car. She stood in the evening, looking at her house. She could see the large windows in front. In her mind, she saw the windows open to show the large, easy rooms inside. The house was built with thought, planning, and love. It was an old house. It was something from the past. But it was part of her life in the present day. Someday, a family she didn't know would live there.

Behind the house, Cecilia saw her three Windspeed wind turbines. Their white blades moved—*whish whish whish*—in the growing darkness. What other changes would Cecilia be lucky enough to see? She didn't know her future.

She had some planning to do.

THE FORAGING CLASS

CHAPTER 1

I was in the kitchen with Mom. It was bright, with early light. I usually loved this combination: kitchen, morning, and sunshine in the window. And Mom being there, of course. Mom (whose name is Alice, in case you wanted to know) loved mornings, too. But not today. I crossed my arms and put my head down. "No," I said. "I'm not going."

"Oh come on, Shana," Mom said. "You'll love it, once you get out there. You'll meet people. We'll be outside."

"Nope," I said again. How many times did I have to say it? No. Nope. No way. Uh-uh. Not going to happen. No. I was not going camping. And I was not going—what did Mom call it—*foraging*?

Mom was quiet for a minute. Then she said, "Well, look, we're going. The foraging class is during spring break. It's a perfect way to enjoy spring. You'll get new energy to finish the school year! We get to camp under the trees, go to the class, and learn how to find wild plants." She pulled up a website on her laptop. I looked at it. I saw: "Foraging Texas," arrow head, lamb's quarter, cat's ear, dollar weed...

"What are these?" I said. The pictures just looked like weeds and grasses.

Mom answered, "These are some of the wild plants we can find and eat!"

My arms were still crossed. "But Kristen wants me to go to Mexico for spring break."

"Shana," Mom said, "I know Kristen asked you, so I called her mother. I had a hard time reaching her. She's very busy. But I did talk to her. She said…"

Mom stopped. Then she spoke softly. "She said they are not going to Mexico."

I dropped my arms and looked up. "What?" I said.

"They are not going to Mexico," Mom said. "It sounds like Kristen's mom and dad aren't doing too well together."

I just looked at Mom.

"In fact," she said, "Kristen's dad left the house. He doesn't live there anymore."

"Oh," I said. "I didn't know. Kristen didn't say anything."

"I think it just happened a few days ago," Mom said.

Suddenly the sunshine didn't seem as bright. I didn't know what to say. I felt bad for Kristen, and surprised, too. Her mom and dad were busy, but they looked happy together. And, I'm afraid I'm not a good person. I did feel bad for Kristen, I really did. But I also felt bad that I wouldn't see Mexico. I didn't know anything about Mexico. But just the idea— another country, and another language! It seemed neat or cool. I felt bad that I had to go to a foraging class, too. How could I tell my friends? I could hear it now. "Hey Shana, where did you go for spring break?" "Uh, I went to a foraging class."

"Shana?" Mom said.

"What?" I said. I didn't like to talk to her that way, just

one word at a time. Alice was great. Alice, that's what I sometimes called her, in my head, but never to her face, of course.

"I have an idea. Let me think about it," Mom said. "We'll talk about this again."

"Yeah," I said. I went to call Kristen.

CHAPTER 2

I saw Kristen for the first time in fifth grade. I loved her little face. She had big eyes, a wide mouth, and bright blond hair. Her feelings were right under her skin. Her little, lovable face changed with every feeling she had, and she had them all.

After hearing the bad news from Mom, I called Kristen. My call was forwarded to voicemail. I didn't waste time, and went over to her house instead. It wasn't far. It was Sunday. Kristen was up, but her mother wasn't. The bedrooms were still dark and quiet.

"Did you get any sleep?" I asked as I gave her a hug. Kristen was still wearing her pajamas.

"Maybe," she said. Then she said, "No." Her little face wobbled. Her wide mouth turned down.

"Are you hungry?" I asked. Kristen didn't answer. She sat down right where we were standing, right down on the kitchen floor.

"Huh!" she said. I went to get some water. She took it and drank it. That gave me an idea. Just a few months ago, Mom let me have my first cup of coffee. She showed me how to make it.

I said to Kristen, "I can make you a cup of coffee!"

"Oh," she said. "Maybe that's a good idea." She stood up off the floor and sat at the kitchen table while I went foraging through the huge kitchen at Kristen's house. I found the coffee, sugar, and milk. In about ten minutes, I handed Kristen a cup of hot coffee.

She tasted it. "Wow," she said.

That's better, I thought. *That's better than sitting on the floor*.

After a few minutes, we started talking about school. Kristen wanted to talk about school, not about her mom and dad. She was working on a project. When we started ninth grade last August, we had to choose one of two classes. One was *home sciences*. Most of the students were girls. They learned how to cook and to sew. The other was *shop*. It had mostly boys. They learned how to build birdhouses and repair cars.

"You don't have a driver's license," Mom said. "How can you repair cars?"

"Next year, Mom," I said.

She put her hand to her head. "Argh," she said.

Kristen took home sciences. I took shop. To my surprise, Kristen loved home sciences, except cooking. She would never be a good cook. But she loved learning to sew. Her first project, a light pink t-shirt, looked great. She made her own design on it with blue and purple thread. My first project, well... it didn't even look like a bird house. Next time, I wanted to build a book rack.

Kristen was talking about her next project. "I just can't get the colors together," she said. "I know what I want the dress to look like—what shape and style. But I can't imagine the colors yet. Dark blue, I guess. But what else? I have to finish right after Spring Break!"

She was quiet for a minute. "I guess I wanted to get some ideas in Mexico. And now..." she stopped talking. Her little face wobbled again. Her light brown eyes looked huge. Her feelings about her dad were right there, under her skin. Was she sad or angry?

I didn't have anything to say. When it came to fathers, I had my own problems.

CHAPTER 3

Spring break was only a week away. Everyone at school was talking about it. My Facebook page was full of posts about spring break—that wonderful ten days of vacation in the middle of March. When you live in Texas, March is the best time for some time off. In case you didn't know, Texas is hot in the summer. I mean really hot, especially in Dallas, where I lived. You didn't really go outside in summer in Texas. You stayed inside and used your computer or texted friends on your cell phone. Maybe after 8 at night you went to someone's pool to meet your friends.

Tilly Gordon was going with her family to the beach in Galveston. They had a vacation house in Galveston. "There'll be college kids there!" Tilly said. I'm sure Mr. and Mrs. Gordon would not let Tilly within one hundred feet of college kids. College students did crazy things during spring break.

Dave Epland was going to Europe. "I don't know exactly where we're going," he said. "Mom's planning it. Paris, maybe?"

Billy Ramirez hit Dave's arm. "You mean Paris, Texas, right?"

"No," Dave said. "Paris, France." Dave and Billy laughed. I laughed along. I hoped no one would ask me where I was going.

Kristen was just as quiet as I was. She told me, "Everyone's so excited about spring break. I don't have to say anything about my mom and dad breaking up."

"Uh-huh," I said. "And I don't have to talk about the foraging class my mom's making me go to."

"Foraging class? What's that?" Kristen asked. She sounded interested.

"We'll drive to east Texas and camp at a state park. Then we'll learn how to find wild plants to eat. Stuff with names like cat's ear and wild onion."

Kristen's brown eyes got very large. "Really?" she said. "Wow…"

"What?" I said. "What do you mean, 'Wow'? I think it's horrible."

"I don't think so," Kristen said. She leaned her head to one side. Her bright blond hair covered her shoulder. "I mean, it could be fun."

I couldn't believe my ears. I was so surprised I couldn't say anything. But, I had an idea. I went home and thought some more. When Mom got home after work, I had a nice pasta dinner ready for her. I even made a fruit salad.

"Whoa," she said. "What's all this?" She looked hungry. She washed her hands and sat down to eat.

"Mom…" I started.

She chewed and swallowed a big bite of pasta. Then she popped an orange slice into her mouth. "Yes, my darling child?"

"Can we ask Kristen to go camping with us? She could take the foraging class with us." I said.

"That's exactly what I was thinking," said Alice, my cool, wonderful Mom. "I already called Kristen's mom and asked her. She said OK."

"What?" I said. For the second time that day, I was completely surprised.

"Yes," Mom said. "I asked Kristen's mom to go, too. But I don't think she'll go."

CHAPTER 4

Kristen stayed at our house the night before we left. We had to leave early the next morning. Mission Tejas State Park, where we would camp, was almost three hours away.

"We're taking only two-lane highways," Mom said. "It might take us a little longer. But it's a more interesting drive. Even Dallas looks more interesting that way."

"Oh," I said, looking at my cell phone. I checked my map app. If we took only two-lane highways, we would go through a lot of little towns, like Kaufman, Athens, and Bois D'Arc. What kind of name was *Bois D'Arc*?

Kristen sat in the back seat. She looked over my shoulder at my phone. "Bois D'Arc?" she said. "What kind of name is that?"

"Sounds French," I said.

"Okay," she said, checking it on her cell phone. "Yep, it's French," she said after a minute. "Bowdark," she said.

"What?" Mom asked.

"It's pronounced bowdark," Kristen said. "It means 'wood for bows'."

"Bows? You mean 'bows' like 'bows and arrows'?" I asked.

"Hmmm," she said. "Not sure." She pushed a few more buttons. "Maybe we can stop in Bois D'Arc and ask someone. There's a restaurant just past there. Coffee?" Kristen looked at me, her eyes wide. I laughed.

Mom drove on. It took a long time to get out of Dallas. We stayed on old U.S. 175, a big two-lane highway. We had to stop for traffic lights. We couldn't go very fast. But by 10 in the morning, we saw a few open fields. Dallas is a huge city. It has dozens of four- and five-lane highways that are always full of cars. One part of Dallas looks like all the other parts— endless shops and houses that look the same. There were "big box" stores every few miles. Today, it was nice to see some open space.

We passed through Kaufman, a small town. Then we passed through Athens, which was a little bigger. Finally, around lunch, we came to Bois D'Arc. There was only one house and one church—nothing else.

"It's like a ghost town," Mom said.

We drove on to the restaurant Kristen found in a town called Palestine.

Palestine, Texas, was a large town. There was a town square with lots of people walking around. They walked into shops, and they stopped to talk to each other. The town square was also filled with beautiful white and pink trees.

"Those are dogwood trees. This is the time of year they blossom," Mom said.

"Wow," Kristen and I said at the same time.

Mom and Kristen looked at the magnificent trees. They were lost in the beautiful pink, white, and cream colors of the blossoms. It was like being in a beautiful dream. But then I noticed a dusty car parked on one side of the town square.

One of its tires was flat. No one could drive around with a flat tire like that. Four women stood around the car talking. I walked over.

"Do you have a flat tire?" I asked. The women looked at me, surprised. Two of the women were older. Their dark, straight, long hair was pulled back. Their eyes were black. The other two women, who were younger, also with long dark hair, both smiled at me.

"Do you know how to change a flat tire?" one of them asked.

CHAPTER 5

There I was in the Palestine, Texas town square, changing a flat tire.

"Where did you learn to do that?" the youngest woman asked. She leaned forward to help. Her straight, dark hair fell over her shoulders.

"Shop class," I said. "At school."

"Oh," she said. "We don't have that in my school. Is it fun?" I wondered where she went to school. She looked the same age as Kristen and me.

The girl had an interesting way of speaking. She spoke English well, but I thought she probably spoke another language. I just couldn't figure out what language.

She told me her name was Kitae'e. She had to say it two or three times. It sounded like *kit-ah-ay*. Finally, she said "Just call me Kitty. It's easier."

Mom and the other three went to get lunch. Kristen stayed to watch me change the tire. In ten minutes, Mom and the women were back with bags of food. I stopped working and ate the most delicious hamburger I ever had. I was hungry. I gave Kristen my coffee. She drank it in about thirty seconds.

"I never knew how much you liked coffee," I said

"Uh-huh," she said, with a sweet smile.

Changing a tire was much harder than I thought. I needed strong hands and wrists to do the job. After a few more minutes more of hard work, an older man and his teenage son stopped to help.

"You're doing all right," the man said. "But the car is moving too much. I'm afraid it might fall. We need to do a few things here and there. Grab that, Stu." He pointed at something. Stu was his son, it seemed.

In another ten minutes, the car tire was changed. The four women thanked the men, and got into their dusty car and drove away. Kitae'e waved out the window. I waved back.

"Thanks, sir, and Stu," I said.

Stu look at me. He was exactly the same height as me. He had deep blue eyes. Then my thoughts sort of stopped. "Uh...." was all I could think. Stu reached over, and gently pulled a dogwood blossom from my hair.

"Ha!" I laughed. Kristen laughed, too.

Stu and his dad said goodbye. Mom had a huge smile on her face. Kristen did, too. What was wrong with everybody? After a minute or two, I went into the restaurant for some iced tea. I also wanted to wash my hands. Changing tires was dirty work. My hands and arms hurt.

We got back into the car and left Palestine with its beautiful dogwood trees and town square. We left its people who were friends to strangers. We left its boy named Stu.

Just south of town, we changed to U.S. Highway 287 and then to a much smaller road, Texas State Highway 294. As we drove along, the trees got taller and taller. They were pines. I had no idea Texas had such pine forests. Mom pulled over so we could see. The pine trees were so tall that the highway looked almost dark. And they smelled wonderful. There is nothing more beautiful than the smell of a pine forest. It was a deep, sharp smell that was sweet and green. I wondered, *Could smells have colors?*

"I didn't know Texas had forests like this," Kristen said. We stood by the side of the road and stared up. "I thought everyplace looked like Dallas."

Finally, Mom said, "This is east Texas. There are pines, for sure."

CHAPTER 6

Mom was driving a little slower. We opened all the car windows. We wanted to drink in the pine forest smell.

"We're just a few minutes from the park," Mom said.

Then, out of nowhere, we saw an open area on the right. There weren't any trees, just an open field. In the middle of the field, there was a steep area. It wasn't a hill, exactly. It was smaller than that and covered in tall grass.

"What in the world?" Mom said, and slowed down even more. A truck honked its horn. "Oops," Mom said. She pulled over, and she smiled and waved at the truck behind us.

The man driving was angry. He put his hands up in a *What are you doing?* gesture. But Alice, my wonderful Mom, just smiled and waved like she had no worries in the world. You would never guess my dad left her when I was only a baby. Actually, I guess he left both of us.

We looked to the other side of the road. It was also an open, grassy field with no trees. We saw grass-covered mounds. Some were gentle and low. Others were steep and very tall. It would be hard to walk on them. There was a line of trees on the far edge of the field, and more trees after that.

Kristen was looking at her cell phone. She said, "The app says there's a state historic site here. Caddo Mounds State Historic Site."

"Oh!" Mom said. "Indian mounds? Here?"

"Yep," Kristen said. "It says they were 'religious centers for the Hasanai Caddo Indians.' And they had a village near here."

"Yes, I see it now," Mom said. "That dark line of trees over there? I think that's a river. This would be a good place for people to live—a good place for a village. But..."

Mom stopped talking. Kristen and I looked at her. "Indian mounds of this kind are very old," she said finally. "Probably something like a thousand years old or more."

Kristen looked at her phone again. "Yes," she said. "1,200 years old. That's what the website says."

"Wow," I said. Then I thought about the four ladies we met.

My face must have changed, because Kristen asked, "What is it?"

"I'm not sure," I said. Then I thought about the four women we met back on the Palestine town square. "I think we might see Kitae'e and her three friends again."

"Why do you think that?" Mom asked.

"I'm pretty sure they're Indians," I said. "But I don't know from which tribe or where they're from. I'm just guessing."

"Their license plate said Oklahoma," Kristen said.

"Oklahoma?" Mom said. "That seems pretty far from Palestine, Texas. And far from here. But you might be right, Shana. Oh, you clever, girl!" She hugged me.

"Mom!" I said, laughing.

"Come on," she said. "Let's get to the park and set up camp." We got into the car. Mom looked for other cars and then pulled out onto the road. Soon, the tall pines crowded in again, and we drove in the dark green, beautiful light.

CHAPTER 7

Just a little later, we arrived at Mission Tejas State Park. We found our campsite. For a few minutes, we just looked straight up into the tall pines. They towered over us. We breathed in that sweet pine smell. The ground was covered with pine needles. We could hear the wind high up in the trees. One bird sang, and then another.

The campground was full because it was spring break. Every student at every school was on vacation. A lot of families used spring break to take trips. It wasn't too hot to sit outside in the spring.

The family across from us was having trouble with their tent. Their three small kids were running around. Every time their mother got the tent up, one of the kids ran right into it and it fell over. Kristen walked over to them. She loved children. She talked to the mother. She played for a little while with the kids and kept them away from the tent.

"My husband's gone for food," the young mother said. She pushed her pretty red hair out of her face.

While Kristen was away from our camp, Mom and I

unloaded the car. We had a large tent and coolers filled with food. I carried over sleeping bags and pillows from the car.

"Mom," I said. "Why do we have four sleeping bags? There's only three of us."

"Shana, come over here," Mom said. "I don't want Kristen to hear."

"Okay," I said. I carried the sleeping bag over to the tent where Mom stood.

She said, "Have you seen how often Kristen looks at her phone?"

"Yes," I said. I remember Kristen looking at her phone a lot on the drive here, but I didn't think anything of it. We all use our phones too much.

"She's worried about her mom," Alice, my wonderful mother, said. Alice always noticed things. "That's only natural. Kristen cares about her mom. Her mom is having a tough time. I called her mom from the restaurant in Palestine. I invited her to meet us at the park again."

"That's great!" I said. "She needs to get away and spend some time here. It's so beautiful."

"Well," Mom said, "I'm not sure she's coming."

"Oh," I said.

"But just in case, we have a sleeping bag for her. You never know, right?"

While we put the tent up, we heard Kristen playing with the kids at the next campsite. The oldest boy, about five, ran straight at Kristen, like he did at the tent. He was no match for Kristen. She was tiny, but she was strong. She held him and laughed. There was no way he could get away. He was a red-faced, red-haired little beast. After a few minutes, the husband showed up with bags of food.

The mother called out, "I got the tent up! Thanks, Kristen!"

"You're welcome!" Kristen said. She walked back to our campsite and said, "They're going to the foraging class, too."

"It won't be quiet with those children! It certainly won't be boring," Mom said. We all laughed.

It started getting dark. It was 5 o'clock. The sun was setting and we were under the trees. The sunset had a red, burning glow to it.

I was wondering if a storm was coming when Mom said, "Looks like there might be a storm."

CHAPTER 8

There was a storm that night. It came after we set up the tent and put our things inside. We also had time to make dinner over a fire. We had delicious tacos. There was so much lettuce and tomato in them they looked like taco salads.

Mom fried some chicken and peppers with spices. I chopped the lettuce and tomatoes. Kristen added garlic to the salsa Mom brought. We piled everything on top of soft corn tortillas. I ate two—I couldn't eat any more. I took some extra over to the family at the next campsite.

The husband bought a lot of candy, chips, and soda, but no real food. "We're going to the foraging class because I want us to eat healthier!" the red-haired woman said. The extra tacos disappeared quickly. They were hungry.

"We'll probably see you over at the class," I said. "It was my mom's idea."

The woman laughed, and handed the empty plate back to me.

I went back to our campsite. We had electricity and water there. We didn't really need the electricity, but we could charge our phones if we needed to. We had flashlights to see at night. We washed our dishes at the water faucet. While we washed them, it got darker and darker. The light turned a strange blue color.

"Here comes the storm," Mom said. "Let's get these dishes finished. We need to check the tent one more time. Listen to that wind!"

She was right. There was a strong wind making the tops of the tall pines creak and sway. The wind sounded like an ocean, or a large rushing river.

We finished the dishes and put them, along with our food, into the car.

"There are a lot of wild animals out here," Mom said. "Deer, coyotes, mice, and raccoons. We don't want them getting into the food." In that strange blue light, we checked the tent. Kristen helped Mom put a large rock under one corner of it. It started to rain.

"Into the tent!" Mom said. The blue light got darker and more blue. Then everything went black as the storm came. The tent shook. The rain hit its sides in big drops, but it seemed fine.

We opened our sleeping bags. We all lay down in the middle of the tent, talking. There was no cell phone service in a storm like this. The rain came down hard. We heard the river of wind, high up in the trees. Suddenly, there was a bright white flash of lightning, and then a crack of thunder. The storm was right on top of us.

"That was close!" Kristen said. Strangely, in the bright flash of the lightning, I could see her smile. She looked excited instead of scared. "This light is amazing," she said. "This is fun!"

Mom laughed. "As long as the tent holds up!" she said.

The tent was fine. We stayed dry. It rained for another hour. The storm moved away. We could still hear rumbles of thunder as it moved east towards Louisiana. It was much colder now.

This is good sleeping weather, I thought. I fell asleep.

Sometime during the night, I woke up. Another storm came, but it stayed to the north of us. I saw the flashes of lightning, and heard a few rumbles of thunder. That storm moved away, too. Mom was asleep, but I could see Kristen's cell phone was on. She was looking for messages from her mother, I guess.

I said, "Kristen, save your phone. With that storm, we might not have electricity tomorrow. You won't be able to charge it up."

She sighed. "I know." She turned her phone off. We talked quietly until we both fell asleep again.

Tomorrow would be the foraging class.

CHAPTER 9

The next morning was foggy. We couldn't see the sun. Instead, the sky went from black to dark gray, then to light gray, and then to silver. The campsites were completely quiet.

I wanted to walk out in this beautiful silver world. I grabbed my towel, soap, and my clothes. I walked through the silver fog to the bath house. I could no longer see our tent. It was swallowed up by the fog.

I saw the pines trees as dark, tall shapes. It was so quiet. The fog made me pay attention to the ground. I had to see what was in front of me. As I walked along the path to the bath house, I saw rocks and pine needles. There was a small stream on my right. The water ran quietly over stones. I stopped and saw a deer at the stream. It was drinking. It looked like a female, a doe. Was there another deer behind her? It looked like it. It was just a moving shape. I waited until the two deer moved off into the fog. Again, except for the stream, the morning was completely silent.

I got to the bath house. I tried not to look at my messy

brown hair in the mirror. None of us could get to the showers last night in the storm.

I looked in the mirror. "Huh," I thought. "It's not that bad. Maybe I should let my hair grow longer." I kept it short. I thought about that boy in Palestine, Texas and the way he pulled the dogwood blossom from my hair. Did he like my hair? I laughed. I washed my hair, combed it out. I put on fresh clothes for the day.

By the time I got back to our campsite, the fog was lifting. Mom and Kristen were waking up. I made three cups of coffee. I got the milk from the cooler and added some to each cup.

Kristen was sitting down and not looking at anything. Her blond hair went in all directions. I put the coffee cup under her nose. Her hands instantly grabbed the cup. *That was easy,* I thought. Mom was still in the tent. I held a coffee cup inside the tent. It immediately disappeared. "Um," I heard Mom say. I drank my coffee sitting on a rock by the stream.

A park ranger stopped by. He saw me and said, "The foraging class begins in 45 minutes. Here's a map. You can walk from here. Don't try to drive your car in this fog. The path starts behind the bath house." He walked to the next campsite. The mother was up, but the kids and father were probably still asleep.

After coffee, both Kristen and Mom woke up a bit more. We were ready to go in fifteen minutes. Mom ate an apple as we walked to the bath house. We found the path through the forest.

"Are you sure this is the right way?" Kristen asked. We were completely surrounded by trees. At one point, we were walking uphill, and then downhill. We crossed a small stream. The fog was still thick under the pine trees, but the path was clear. It led straight ahead.

After five minutes, we could see brighter light. We came out into the field we saw from the road the day before. The fog was completely gone. We saw lots of green, grassy, steep mounds. They stretched away as far as we could see.

Mom said, "There's the foraging class." She pointed.

There they were, five or six people standing at the edge of the trees, waiting for us. One of them was Kitae'e.

CHAPTER 10

I was glad to see Kitae'e. She waved hello, and Kristen and I went over to her.

"Hey!" I said.

"Hi," Kitae'e said. "I had no idea you were coming here. It's great to see you!"

Again, I liked the interesting way she spoke. English was not her first language, even though she spoke easily. *From Oklahoma?* I thought.

As we talked, her three friends came out of the forest. They walked into the field. One of them, the oldest woman, stopped and looked at the grasses at the edge of the field. She bent over and picked something up. It was green. Was it a leaf?

The women still had the same straight, dark, long hair and the same black eyes. But their clothes—they wore long dresses in dark blue, purple, pink, white, orange, green, yellow. There were so many colors that I lost count! They put colors together in such interesting ways.

The younger woman wore a light blue dress with purple

and red and white designs on it. She pulled her hair back with a wide blue, yellow, and white cloth. The oldest woman wore a purple dress with green, black, light blue, and brown stripes across her back. At the bottom of the dress were the same colors, like a rainbow. But no rainbow ever held colors together in this way. It was amazing! These women put together light blues, oranges, purples, and browns, and it worked.

Kristen was standing very still. She was looking at those dresses with their beautiful colors. I could see what she was thinking. She saw how the colors were put together, and how interesting they looked. Seeing Kristen now was like seeing her during the storm the night before. Her little face glowed in the flashes of the lightning. She was excited and enjoying it.

"What is it?" Kitae'e asked, watching Kristen. She sounded worried.

Kristen didn't answer. She was too busy enjoying the women's dresses.

"Kristen loves clothes. You have no idea," I said. "She was working on a dress for a school project. Right now, she's thinking about how beautiful and interesting all those colors are together. She loves the dresses your friends are wearing!"

Kitae'e relaxed a little. Then she said, "Well, that's my grandmother," she pointed. "She's Margaret Deer. And that is my aunt. Her name is Edith Kichai. And the girl is my cousin. She's Pichita Kichai. Those dresses are their ceremonial clothes."

That got Kristen's attention. She asked, "Ceremonial clothes? You mean clothes for something religious?"

"Yes," Kitae'e said. "They're teaching me now. We have to make our own dresses."

I looked at Kitae'e. I took in her smooth brown skin and

her beautiful straight black hair. I took a breath and asked, "I'm just curious. Could you tell me where you're from? And why you're here now?"

"Well," she said, "we live in Oklahoma now. But a hundred years ago, we were from here. We're Caddo Indians."

"Ohhh," Kristen and I said together.

I had a thousand questions, but my questions would have to wait. The foraging class was beginning.

CHAPTER 11

The ranger from Mission Tejas State Park talked to us about foraging. He said, "Foraging for food is something every group of people and every culture has done. It's a very old practice. I think you'll enjoy it. This is a great time of year to forage. Lots of plants are growing with the warm weather. They're tender and delicious to eat now."

He handed out cards with pictures and names of plants we could find to eat. On the cards, I could see many of the plants from the "Foraging Texas" website that Mom showed me.

The ranger started talking again. "Arrowhead grows near or in water. Its young leaves are good to eat in the spring, too."

I kept reading. Next, there was *cat's ear*.

"It looks like a dandelion with flat green leaves and bright yellow flowers. Cat's ear's leaves are long and pointed with little teeth, like little knives. Its young leaves are best to eat in the spring, too."

The ranger let us study the cards for a few minutes. Then he put us into groups of three. Mom, Kristen, and I were in one group. Kitae'e, her aunt, and her cousin were in another. An older husband and wife were in the third group with their young grandson. The tired, red-haired mom from the campsite next to us was by herself. We invited her to come with us. She looked happy. She said, "I couldn't wake anyone up in our camp. The storm kept them up late, so I came by myself."

Kristen looked at me. She loved kids, but this morning, it was nice to have a little quiet. I looked around for Margaret Deer, Kitae'e's grandmother. She stood near a mound far from us. Her hands were up in the air. I thought she was talking. I couldn't see clearly, though.

Mom said, "Come on Shana. We're starting." She saw who I was looking at. Then she said, "I think she may be praying." Then she took my hand and we joined our group.

The park ranger made the groups move about fifty feet apart. He asked each group to walk in a straight line. We started from the field, and walked into the deep grass. Our path took us into the forest. He said that in about five minutes, we would come to a river. As we walked along, we should look only for the plants we saw on the cards. The ranger was clear.

He said, "Don't pick anything yet. Remember where you find the plants. I will come to your group, and we will walk back to the field together. I want to check what you think you found. And then, if I say so, you can pick some plants to take with you."

It was a beautiful day. The fog was gone. The sky was clear. It wasn't too hot yet. While we were still in the tall grass, we found wild onions. Mom rubbed the tall green and white flower and then sniffed her fingers.

"Yep, that's onion," she said. We walked into the forest along our "line." There, we found a carpet of dollar weed—

short green plants. They looked exactly like small green coins. The leaves were perfectly round.

"I hear water!" said the red-headed mom. Sure enough, in less than a minute, we came to a beautiful little river. Right in front of us we saw a lot of long, green, sharp looking leaves. They grew straight out of the water.

"Arrowhead," Mom said.

It was amazing. Once we knew what to look for, the plants were everywhere. It was like finding a new world, one that was invisible before. We waited for the ranger. We listened to a light wind in the trees. We listened to the river talk to us. We smelled the beautiful pine trees.

CHAPTER 12

We spent the rest of the morning walking back to the mound field with the park ranger. As we walked back along our path, we picked arrowhead leaves, dollar weed, and cat's ear. We had a bag for each. The ranger told us, "Make sure you don't pick all the plants in one spot. Leave a few to grow back."

The tired, red-headed woman didn't look as tired now. She looked relaxed, and her face had a little more color. I think she needed a morning off.

Kristen was quiet. She didn't check her cell phone once. She looked relaxed, just like the red-headed mom without the three kids. Alice, too, my wonderful mother, smiled. She stopped from time to time to look at dollar weed or cat's ear.

When all the groups met up with the park ranger, we compared our foraging bags.

Kitae'e, her aunt, and cousin found some plants we didn't have.

"Yes," said the park ranger. "This is burdock. It's very good in salads."

"It's hard to find this in Oklahoma," said Pichita Kichai,

Kitae'e's cousin. "It's too dry where we are. Our people ate this a lot, I think, when we still lived here." She sounded like Kitae'e. She had very good English, but her way of speaking was different. Her mouth never completely closed.

The foraging class ended. The park ranger gave us some ideas on how to use our leaves in salads and soups. He wanted to make sure we washed everything carefully before we ate it.

The red-headed woman went back to the park. She used the same forest path we used that morning. She said, "We're probably leaving today. So if I don't see you again, thank you. It was fun being in class with you, and all."

"Mom, let's go back too," I said. "I'm hungry."

Mom didn't move. She was looking at a big mound in the center of the field. It was far away. Kristen stood next to her. I went to see what they were looking at.

Kitae'e, Margaret Deer, Edith, and Pichita Kichai were walking around the mound. I could see Margaret Deer's dark blue, orange, and green dress. Every few feet, the Caddo Indians stopped. They raised their hands in the air. We could hear something like a song. Finally, they disappeared on the far side of the mound.

"What are they doing?" Kristen asked.

"Something religious?" I said. "Their people came from here. Maybe they built the mounds." We watched a few more minutes, and I finally said, "I don't know."

Finally, the four Caddo women came around the mound. They walked towards us. We didn't want them to know we were watching them. We turned away a little, but when they got close enough, Kitae'e waved.

She called out, "Don't leave yet! My grandmother wants to meet you."

CHAPTER 13

"Ah!" Mom said.

"Wow," Kristen said. "I was starting to think the other women would never talk."

"Yeah," I said. "Tell me about it."

"Shhh, now," Mom said. "Here they come." Since I now had two thousand questions, I knew just listening would be hard to do.

Kitae'e said, "My grandmother, Margaret Deer, wants to meet you."

"Of course," Mom said. "Happy to meet you."

"Happy to meet you," Kristen and I said together.

Margaret Deer came very close to us. She looked us over. When she looked at me, I felt a little shaky. Her eyes were very dark. I couldn't read her face, but when she stepped back to talk to us, she was just a very short woman wearing a beautiful dress.

Kitae'e said, "Margaret Deer does not speak English very often. It's not her way. So I will translate for her." Then she said something to Margaret Deer I couldn't understand.

Margaret Deer started to talk. It was like hearing a song. Her sentences were long. Her voice was high. She stopped, and it became very quiet.

Kitae'e had a funny look on her face. Then she said, "Margaret Deer thinks that one of you is missing someone. One of you feels sad."

"What?" I asked. Surely I could ask just one question. I still had 1,999 to go!

"She said, 'The person you are longing for may still come. Don't give up. Enjoy the night. Watch for the deer. Watch for the coyotes. Watch for all the gifts of this place. Don't be afraid. That's all," Kitae'e said. She still had that funny look on her face.

Margaret Deer reached over and patted Kristen's arm. She smiled.

We stood in complete silence as we watched the Caddo women walk to their dusty car. I could see it by the side of the road past the last mound. I waved to Kitae'e when she turned around. She waved back.

We didn't say much. We walked back to Mission Tejas State Park on the forest path. When we got back to our campsite, the family next to us was gone. Mom barely noticed. Kristen sat down and didn't even look at her cell phone.

We washed our arrowhead leaves and our dollar weed. Mom made a kind of salad. It was good. We tried some of the cat's ear, which was spicy and peppery. There was too much for our salad. Mom pulled out a big bag of corn chips. And then, somehow, we all started talking at once. We were all smiling and couldn't stop.

We ate the crunchy corn chips and our fresh salad. We talked the whole time.

Finally Mom said, "We have flashlights. Why don't we walk out to the mounds tonight?"

"Yeah!" Kristen and I answered.

Above us, the tall pine trees moved slowly back and forth.

CHAPTER 14

It got dark early this time of year. It was only 6 o'clock when the sun went down, and a full moon started to rise. We got ready for our walk to the Caddo Mounds. It was cold, and we wore jackets and long pants. Kristen wore pink sneakers, and I wore pink gloves with glitter on them. They were a surprise gift from Kristen.

"I put the glitter on myself," she said when she gave them to me last Christmas. The glitter shone like ice in the moonlight. We each carried a flashlight.

The fog was coming in again. Tonight, it stayed low to the ground. As we walked to the bath house along the small stream, I saw little fingers of fog rising up from the water. We walked through the woods past the bath house. We turned on our flashlights. Except for the trees moving a little, far above us, it was completely quiet. Mom, at the front of the group, stopped.

"I don't think you're going to need your flashlights," she said. She was right. The moon was bright above us. We turned off our flashlights.

We came out of the trees and onto the field where the Caddo Mounds were. We gazed out on the field together. A low, white fog covered the field. It reflected the moonlight like a silver carpet. Only the mounds rose above the fog.

Something moved, far on our left. I said as quietly as I could, "Mom, look... over there."

A deer came out of the forest. She walked out onto the field. Then she bent her head down to eat some of the new green grass. A second deer, also female, came out of the forest. She looked right at us. None of us breathed. Then she moved on, into the field. Two more young deer followed them. We counted four deer. They had white tails and long brown legs. They looked up and around, and then they ate more grass. They moved slowly off behind one mound.

The wind picked up a little. We heard it in the forest behind us. It sounded like rushing water. The fog shifted ahead of us. Then we heard something new. It sounded like a dog, but dogs didn't sound like that. It sounded like a high song. It howled and then stopped. Then it started again. It went higher and higher. Then we heard an answer from the other side of the field.

"Coyotes," Mom said.

In a few minutes, we heard a third howl, then a fourth. The first coyote, the one closest to us, barked from nearby. We froze.

"Coyotes won't hurt us," Mom said. "Let's just see what happens. Don't be scared."

"I'm not scared," Kristen whispered. "Do you think we'll see any?"

Just then, a coyote trotted out onto the field. It looked like a medium-sized dog. We could see its gray fur and its white muzzle. It looked back at us for a second, and then it kept trotting. In another minute, it was joined by three more coyotes. As the fog thinned and came apart, we could see the four coyotes playing together. They weren't close to us, but we could see them jumping and running around. One of them gave a final howl and another answered. Then they disappeared into the darkness.

We stayed a few more minutes. Then it got colder, and it was time to go.

CHAPTER 15

When we got back to our campsite, we started a fire. It was cold. We wanted to warm up before crawling into our sleeping bags. We could just barely see the bright moon through the tops of the trees.

As we sat in the orange glow of the fire, Mom said, "Shana, Kristen, I don't know what we saw tonight. What do you think we saw?"

I answered, "Deer and coyotes live here. We should expect to see them. I think we were just lucky. I never saw a coyote before. I always just hear them. They're afraid of us."

Kristen was quiet for a minute. Then she said, "Whatever we saw, I'm not sure I want to tell anyone. It was special. Margaret Deer told us to watch for them. It was a gift. She didn't have to meet us at all. We're just some white people from a world that doesn't even know about the Caddo Indians."

"Gee, Kristen," I said. I was about to make a joke about how she was talking more now than she had all week. But somehow, I didn't think that was the right thing to say. Kristen had deep feelings.

"Girls," Mom said, pointing. We saw the headlights of a car coming from the park entrance. "Kristen, is that your…"

Kristen stood up in a flash. She waited for the car to stop at our campsite. There she was—Kristen's mom. She came after all.

"Mom!" Kristen said. "You came!"

In about two seconds, Kristen's mother was out of the car. She hugged Kristen. After a few more minutes of hugging and crying, Kristen and her mother hugged us. We showed her to her sleeping bag. It was right where we laid it out on the very first day.

The next morning, I got to make four cups of coffee. Around lunchtime, we all said goodbye. Kristen went home with her mom. They both had huge smiles.

Alice and I never got to use the cat's ear on our trip. Instead, we took it home in our cooler. On the night we got home, we put it into some pasta that Mom made. We added a little cheese and a little butter. It tasted great. That cat's ear was sharp, peppery, and just what we wanted.

"No Facebook tonight?" Mom asked. She was used to my logging on before dinner was over.

"What?" I said. "Maybe." What would I say about spring break? There was Stu, of Palestine, Texas…

After I helped wash the dishes, I went into our back yard. Night was coming. We had grass, and a few small trees. I never spent much time out there. It was more an idea of a yard than a real yard.

As I thought about our trip, the foraging class, Kitae'e, the deer, and everything else, I heard the first cricket of the season begin to sing. *"Reep....reep reep,"* it said. I went over to a tree to see if I could find it. In the last bit of sunset, I saw some dollar weed. Their green leaves were round like coins. Then I saw a larger bunch of dollar weed. There it was, right in my back yard.

"Yes," I said. "Yes, yes, uh-huh, yep, yeah, and yes."

BOOKS IN THIS SERIES

American Chapters books by Greta Gorsuch

- *The Bee Creek Blues & Meridian*
- *Lights at Chickasaw Point & The Two Garcons*
- *Living at Trace*
- *Summer in Cimarron & Lunch at the Dixie Diner*
- *The Storm*
- *Cecilia's House & The Foraging Class*

Ebooks and paperbacks are available from your favorite online retailer. Paperbacks may also be ordered by any bookstore, using the ISBN. For more information, including store links, please see our website at

http://wayzgoosepress.com/greta-gorsuch